scribbles noted   9-19 /cw

DATE DUE			
FEB 07 2011		NOV 23 2009	
AUG 14 2011		SEP 11 2010	
JUL 10 2012			
OCT 11 2012		JUN 25 2013	

My Car

12-95 midwest 12.99

For a free color catalog describing Gareth Stevens' list of high-quality books, call 1-800-542-2595 (USA) or 1-800-461-9120 (Canada). Gareth Stevens' Fax: (414) 225-0377.

Library of Congress Cataloging-in-Publication Data

Davies, Kay.
    My car / by Kay Davies and Wendy Oldfield ; photographs by Fiona Pragoff.
       p. cm. — (First step science)
    Includes bibliographical references and index.
    ISBN 0-8368-1185-2
    1. Automobiles—Juvenile literature. 2. Automobiles— Models—Experiments—Juvenile literature.
[1. Automobiles. 2. Science—Experiments. 3. Experiments.] I. Oldfield, Wendy. II. Pragoff, Fiona,
ill. III. Title. IV. Series.
TL147.D38 1995
530—dc20
                                        94-34038

This edition first published in 1995 by
Gareth Stevens Publishing
1555 North RiverCenter Drive, Suite 201
Milwaukee, Wisconsin 53212, USA

This edition © 1995 by Gareth Stevens, Inc. Original edition published in 1991 by A & C Black (Publishers) Ltd., 35 Bedford Row, London WC1R 4JH. © 1991 A & C Black (Publishers) Ltd. Photographs © 1991 Fiona Pragoff. Additional end matter © 1995 by Gareth Stevens, Inc.

Series editor: Patricia Lantier-Sampon
Editorial assistants: Mary Dykstra, Diane Laska
Illustrations: Mandy Doyle
Science consultant: Dr. Bryson Gore

Printed in the United States of America
1 2 3 4 5 6 7 8 9 99 98 97 96 95

First Step Science

My Car

by Kay Davies and Wendy Oldfield
photographs by Fiona Pragoff

Gareth Stevens Publishing
MILWAUKEE

Look at all these cars. How many can you see?

What colors and shapes are they?

This is my favorite car.

My car has four wheels.

The wheels go around
fast when I spin them.

My car goes backward and forward
in a straight line.

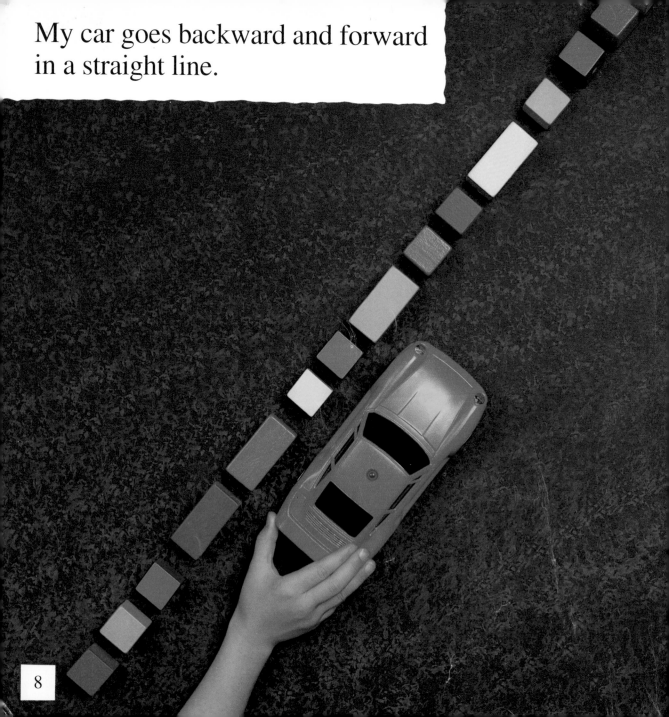

I can steer my car
around corners.

9

It's easy to push my car on the table.

But on the carpet, it's much harder.
I can feel all the bumps.

In dry sand, my car gets stuck.

But in damp sand, the wheels roll along easily.

They make tracks in the sand.

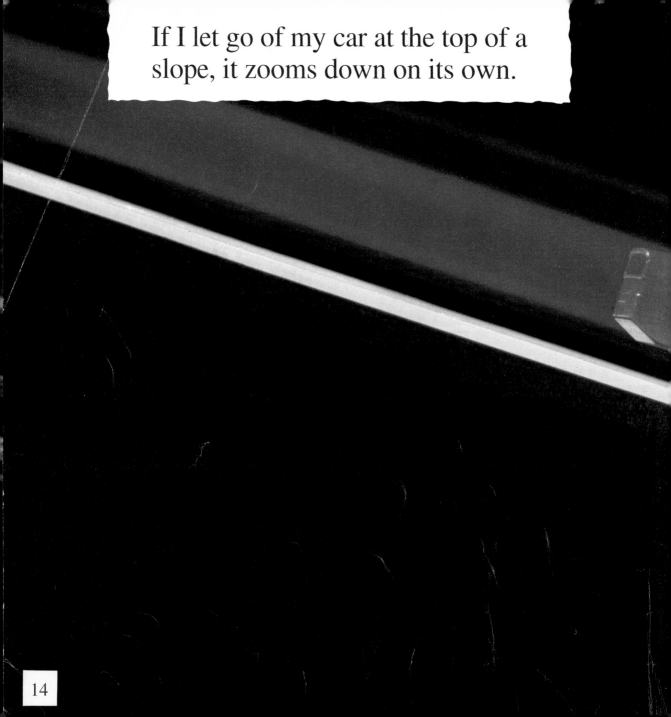

If I let go of my car at the top of a slope, it zooms down on its own.

What will happen if I make the slope steeper?

Whoops! My car has hit a wall.

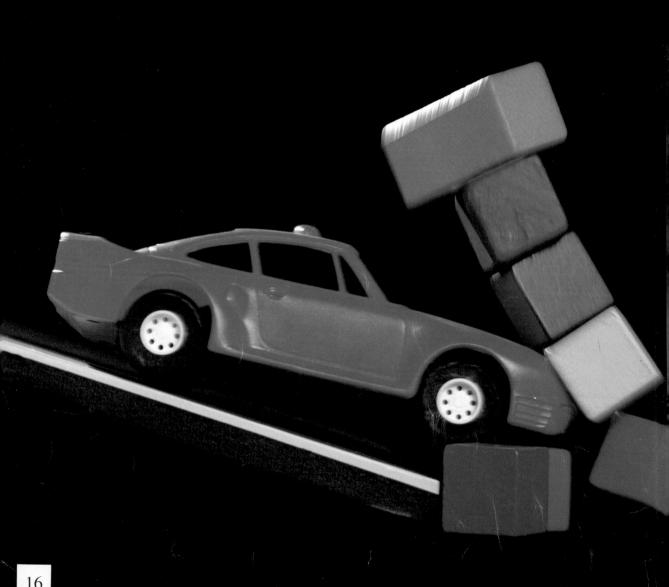

Which car will get to the bottom first?

Georgina's plastic truck is huge. But my small, metal car is heavier.

My car sinks in water. Do you think the truck will sink, too?

Now my car floats!

We're making a truck.
Reuben is attaching wheels.

21

I'm painting our truck.

23

Which car will win this race?

FOR MORE INFORMATION

Notes for Parents and Teachers

As you share this book with young readers, these notes may help you explain the scientific concepts behind the different activities.

pages 4, 5, 21, 22, 24, 25
Colors and shapes

Cars can be sorted into different groups according to color or shape. Fast cars are a streamlined shape to reduce the amount of air resistance pulling against the cars and slowing them down.

pages 6, 7, 8, 9, 21 Wheels

Wheels roll over surfaces, reducing the amount of friction that occurs when two surfaces rub against each other. Friction is a force that tends to slow down objects and stop their movement. A stationary wheel needs an outside force to make it move. It will keep moving until another force makes it change its speed or direction of movement.

pages 10, 11, 12, 13
Rough and smooth

There is more friction on a rough, uneven surface, such as a carpet, than on a smooth surface. Wheels won't turn easily in dry sand because the sand offers little resistance for the wheels to push against. Car wheels need some friction to help them grip the road. Tire treads help wheels grip wet, icy, or muddy roads.

pages 14, 15, 17
Sliding down slopes

The force of gravity pulls the car

down the slope. The force of gravity is stronger on a steeper slope, and the car moves faster.

page 16 Stopping cars
A force is needed to make a car stop moving. In this case, some of the energy in the moving car is transferred to the bricks in the wall, which makes them fly up into the air.

page 18 How heavy?
The mass or weight of something depends not only on its size but also on the materials it is made from. The large plastic truck is lighter than the small metal car.

pages 19, 20
Floating and sinking
The metal car is heavier or more dense than water, so the car sinks in water. By putting the car on a piece of Styrofoam, which is much less dense than water, the car floats.

pages 21, 22 Making a truck
The truck on these pages is made from cardboard boxes, dowels (for the axles), and empty thread spools (for the wheels). The spools are attached to the dowels with modeling clay so they will turn around when the axle turns. Encourage the children to experiment with different designs and materials.

page 23 Carrying loads
More objects can be fitted into a truck if the load is packed evenly. If the shapes fit closely together or settle, even more objects can fit into a small space. By filling trucks with marbles and counting the number of marbles, the volumes of different trucks can be compared.

Things to Do

1. All sorts of wheels

See how many different kinds of wheels you can find. How big are the wheels? What are they made from? Try to find some gear wheels that have teeth around the edges. What are gear wheels used for?

2. Patterns and tracks

Gather a group of toy cars and trucks that have different tire patterns. Roll out a sheet of modeling clay until it is as flat as possible. To make a record of different tire patterns, press the wheels firmly into the modeling clay. Can you think of other objects that make tracks?

3. Car catalog

Cut out several different pictures of cars, trucks, and vans from old magazines. How many different ways can you classify, or group, your pictures? For example, you might classify the vehicles by color or the number of doors. After sorting the vehicles into the various categories you have chosen, glue the pictures into a notebook to make your own car catalog.

4. Getting going

Attach an elastic band to one of your toy cars and pull it along a smooth surface. Does the elastic band stretch before your car starts to move? Does it stretch more or less when the car is moving? Try this on rougher surfaces such as grass, gravel, or pavement. Is there a difference?

Fun Facts about Cars

1. The first cars were called "horseless carriages."

2. Race cars travel very fast, and their tires need to be changed during long races. A pit crew with fourteen people can change a car's four tires in less than ten seconds.

3. Computers test car engines. The computers can determine if any parts of a car need to be repaired or replaced.

4. Although most cars have gas engines, there are also battery-operated electric cars. Some scientists are also experimenting with solar-powered cars, using energy from the sun to charge a large battery.

5. The first cars used in the early 1900s had oil lamps to provide light for nighttime driving, instead of the convenient headlights cars have today.

6. Gravity is the force that pulls objects down a slope. A car has an emergency brake to keep it from rolling when it is parked on a slope.

7. A stretch limousine made in 1989 had room for fifteen passengers. This special car had four television sets and two whirlpool tubs!

8. About one-tenth of a car's total weight is made of plastic that can be recycled.

Glossary

attach — to fasten one object onto another, such as fastening two pieces of paper together with a paper clip.

bottom — the lowest point of something.

damp — moist; a little wet.

float — to stay or rest on the surface of a liquid.

heavier — weighing more than something else.

marbles — small, colorful glass balls used to play games.

plastic — a material made from chemicals that can easily be molded or shaped.

sand — tiny grains of loose rock.

sink — to fall below the surface of a liquid.

slope — an upward slant, such as the side of a mountain.

spin — to rotate, or quickly move around a central point.

steeper — having a higher slope.

steer — to control the direction in which something moves.

stuck — to be in a position that allows no freedom of movement.

tracks — footprints or other identifying marks made in a soft surface, such as sand or mud.

wheels — round objects that turn around a central point.

zoom — to move very quickly.

Places to Visit

Everything we do involves some basic scientific principles. Listed below are a few museums that offer a variety of scientific information and experiences. You may also be able to locate other museums in your area. Just remember: you don't always have to visit a museum to experience the wonders of science. Science is everywhere!

The Smithsonian Institution
1000 Jefferson Drive SW
Washington, D.C. 20560

Canadian Automotive Museum
99 Simcoe Street S
Oshawa, Ontario
L1H 4G7

The Exploratorium
3601 Lyon Street
San Francisco, CA 94123

Henry Ford Museum
Village Road and
     Oakwood Boulevard
Dearborn, MI 48121

Craven Foundation Automobile
     Museum
780 Lawrence Avenue W
Toronto, Ontario M6A 1B8

More Books to Read

Amazing Cars
     Trevor Lord (Knopf)

An Auto Mechanic
     Douglas Florian (Greenwillow)

Cars
Ian Graham
(Steck-Vaughn)

Things on Wheels
Jerry Young
(Covent Garden)

The Science Book of Gravity
Neil Ardley
(Harcourt Brace Jovanovich)

Things That Go
Lara Tankel Holtz
(Dorling Kindersley)

Videotapes

Cars, Boats, Trains, and Planes
(Kidsongs/Warner Bros.)

My First Science Video
(Sony)

Index